Aunt Nina, Good Night

by FRANZ BRANDENBERG • pictures by ALIKI

 GREENWILLOW BOOKS, NEW YORK

Watercolor paints, colored pencils, and a black pen were used
for the full-color art. The text type is Baskerville.

Library of Congress Cataloging-in-Publication Data
Brandenberg, Franz.
Aunt Nina, goodnight / by Franz Brandenberg; pictures by Aliki.   p.   cm.
Summary: When Aunt Nina's nephews and nieces spend the night, they
find a multitude of excuses for not going to sleep right away.
ISBN 0-688-07463-4.   ISBN 0-688-07464-2 (lib. bdg.)
[1. Bedtime—Fiction. 2. Aunts—Fiction.]   I. Aliki, ill.   II. Title.
PZ7.B7364Aub 1989   [E]—dc19   88-18777   CIP   AC

Printed in Hong Kong by South China Printing Co.

For the dearest aunt ever—
Minerva Theodos
and her grandchildren
Christina Nicole
and
Dean Alexander

Aunt Nina invited her nephews and nieces
to spend the night.

After dinner the nephews and nieces got
undressed in no time.

"Lights out!" Aunt Nina said to the nephews.

"Lights out!" she said to the nieces.

"We miss our sisters," cried the nephews.
"We miss our brothers," cried the nieces.
"You can all sleep in my bed," said Aunt Nina.
"Great!" said the nephews and nieces.

"Lights out!" said Aunt Nina.

"We miss our parents," cried the nephews
and nieces.

"Let's call them," said Aunt Nina.

"Great!" said the nephews and nieces.

"Lights out!" said Aunt Nina.
"We miss Fluffy," cried the nephews and
nieces.
"She doesn't miss you," said Aunt Nina.
"Boo-hoo!" said the nephews and nieces.

"Lights out!" said Aunt Nina.
"You forgot to read us a story," said the
nephews and nieces.
"I'll read you one right now," said Aunt Nina.
"Great!" said the nephews and nieces.

"Lights out!" said Aunt Nina.
"The curtains are blowing," cried the nephews
and nieces.
"I'll pull them back," said Aunt Nina.
"Great!" said the nephews and nieces.

"Lights out!" said Aunt Nina.

"The clock is ticking," cried the nephews and
nieces.

"I'll stop it," said Aunt Nina.

"Great!" said the nephews and nieces.

"Lights out!" said Aunt Nina.
"We forgot to say good night to the rabbits,"
 cried the nephews and nieces.
"Go do it now," said Aunt Nina.
"Great!" said the nephews and nieces.

"Lights out!" said Aunt Nina.
"We aren't sleepy," said the nephews and
  nieces.
"Let's have a pillow fight," said Aunt Nina.
"Great!" said the nephews and nieces.

"Lights out!" said Aunt Nina.

"We miss Aunt Nina," cried the nephews and
nieces.

"I miss my nephews and nieces," said Aunt
Nina.

She climbed into bed with them.

"Lights out!" said the nephews.
"Good night!" said the nieces.
"Sleep tight!" said Aunt Nina.